Hans Christian Andersen
THE EMPEROR'S NEW CLOTHES

Retold by
Ned Bustard

Illustrated by
Matthew Clark

"So why do you worry about clothing? Consider the lilies of the field, how they grow: they neither toil nor spin;
and yet I say to you that even Solomon in all his glory was not arrayed like one of these." MATTHEW 6:28-29

This story is lovingly dedicated to my sister, Melissa—who knows the difference between a swindle and a bargain when she sees it.
—NB—

These illustrations are dedicated to my wife, Amy—who is never afraid to tell me when my Emperor has no clothes.
—MC—

Copyright ©2004 Veritas Press
www.VeritasPress.com
ISBN 978-1-932168-22-8

Fabric photos by www.SAGordon.com
Printed in the United States of America.

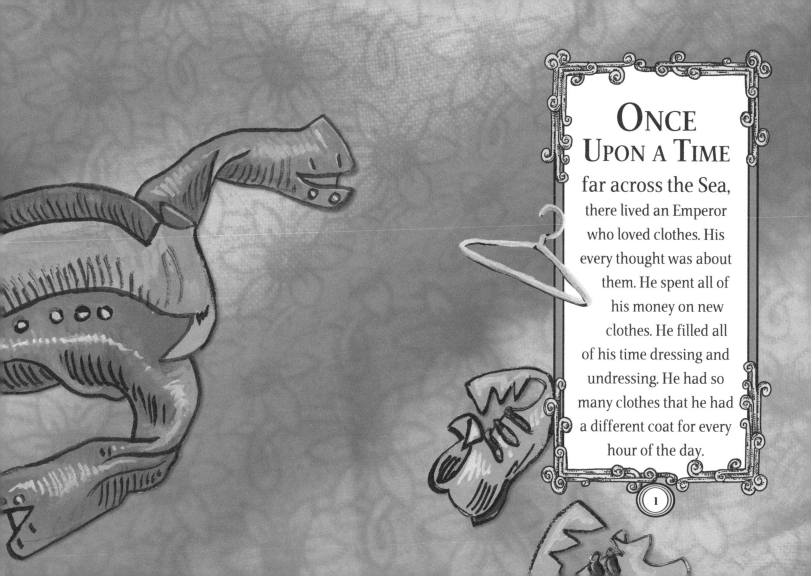

ONCE UPON A TIME

far across the Sea, there lived an Emperor who loved clothes. His every thought was about them. He spent all of his money on new clothes. He filled all of his time dressing and undressing. He had so many clothes that he had a different coat for every hour of the day.

1

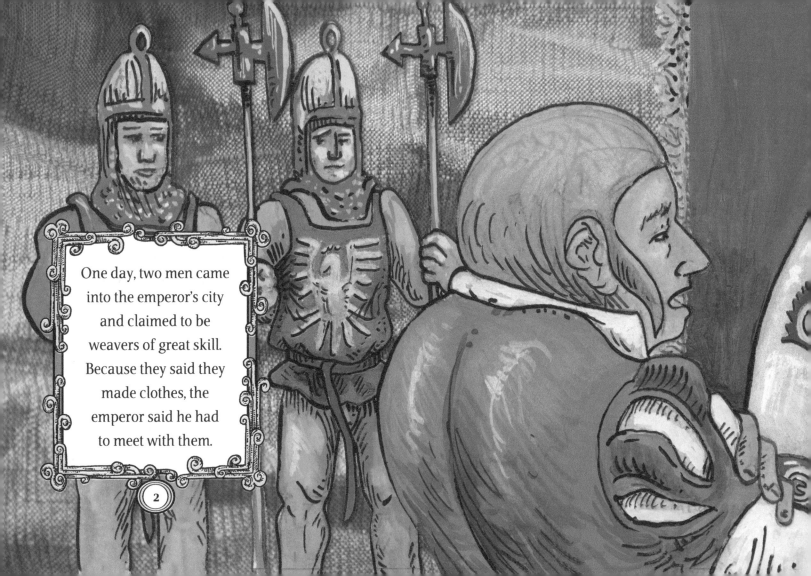

One day, two men came into the emperor's city and claimed to be weavers of great skill. Because they said they made clothes, the emperor said he had to meet with them.

2

"Your Majesty," said the first man, "We have traveled from distant lands with the humble hope of crafting clothes for the man known far and wide as the smartest dressed of all royalty." "We make uncommonly beautiful fabric," the other man added. "The color and pattern is woven so that it seems to be invisible to any man who is unfit for his work —or is simply stupid."

3

"*What grand clothing that must be!*" thought the emperor. "*If I possessed such finery I would be able to stroll through my empire and easily separate the brilliant from the buffoon.*" The emperor was so excited with the idea of the magical cloth that he gave a large sum of money to the weavers so they could begin working that very day.

4

Yet the two men were not weavers, but thieves. They ordered two huge weaving looms built on the emperor's estate and called for supplies of the finest silk and the best gold. The gold and silk they hid away to profit from later. On the empty looms they worked until late into the night, pretending to be very busy with the warp and woof—though there were no threads ever woven.

The emperor waited days and days for the magic fabric. *"I am eager to learn how the weavers are coming with the cloth,"* thought the emperor. Yet every time he started to check on the weavers, he would change his mind, for he would recall mistakes he had made as emperor and realized the cloth might reveal him to be unworthy to be the emperor.

6

Since the cloth uncovered those unfit for their jobs, he thought it wise to send someone else first to see how the weaving went. "I will ask my oldest and wisest adviser to make the visit," the emperor finally decided. "He can judge best how it looks, for he is intelligent and no one is more worthy of his job."

By now everyone in the city had heard of the peculiar power that the magnificent fabric was said to possess and all were anxious to see it so they might see how stupid their neighbors were.

So when the adviser arrived, his eyes grew wide as he stared at the empty looms. *"Goodness gracious me!"* thought the old man, *"I cannot see any cloth at all! Could I be unfit for my work? Am I stupid?"* The cheats invited the old adviser to come near. While pointing to the empty looms they asked him if he admired the exquisite pattern and the beautiful colors.

The old man tried his best, but he could see nothing —for of course there was nothing to be seen. He thought, *"I must not say that I cannot see the cloth, or the emperor will take away my job."*
"Have you no comment?" asked one of the weavers. "Oh, it ... is ... very ... pretty—quite enchanting!" replied the old minister, while peering through his thick glasses.

"What a beautiful pattern, what brilliant colors! I will report to the emperor that I found the cloth very charming."

"We are pleased to hear that," said the weavers, winking to each other. Then they described all the varied colors and curious patterns. The old adviser listened attentively, so he might recite to the emperor exactly what the weavers said.

11

Not long after the old adviser's visit, the thieves informed the emperor that their supplies were running low. They insisted that they needed more silk and gold for weaving. Upon receiving more supplies, they once again hid the precious materials and continued to work on the empty looms as before. Still the emperor had seen no finished fabric, and the weeks were passing by.

So he sent his most honest courtier to the weavers to see how their work was progressing. The honest courtier looked and looked but could see nothing, for, again, there was nothing to be seen. "Is it not a beautiful piece of cloth?" asked the two devious men as they pretended to show off the magnificent material.

"*I am not stupid,*"
thought the honest
courtier. "*I must be unfit
for my good office. It is
very strange because
I thought I did my job well.
Regardless, I must not let
anyone know it.*"
So the once-honest
courtier praised the cloth
he could not see—and
expressed marvel at the
colors and patterns.
"It is very excellent,"
he later informed
the emperor.

14

Everyone in the city was buzzing about the cloth being crafted for the emperor. High and low, the only thing spoken of was the fabric that was invisible to anyone who was unfit for his work— or just plain stupid.

The emperor could wait no longer. He insisted on seeing the fabric himself. He brought along all of his most important statesmen, including the honest courtier and the old adviser.

The cunning criminals were, by then, very skilled at pretending to weave with passion and intensity, though without fiber or thread. "Is it not splendid?" led out the honest courtier. "Your Majesty must admire the fine pattern and the colors?" asked the old adviser. And they both pointed at the empty loom, for they thought that all the others must be able to see the clever cloth laid out in all its glory.

"This is the most horrible thing that could ever happen to me" thought the emperor. *"I cannot see any cloth! Am I unfit to be emperor? Am I stupid?"* He said aloud, "Err, yes, indeed … it is very pretty!"

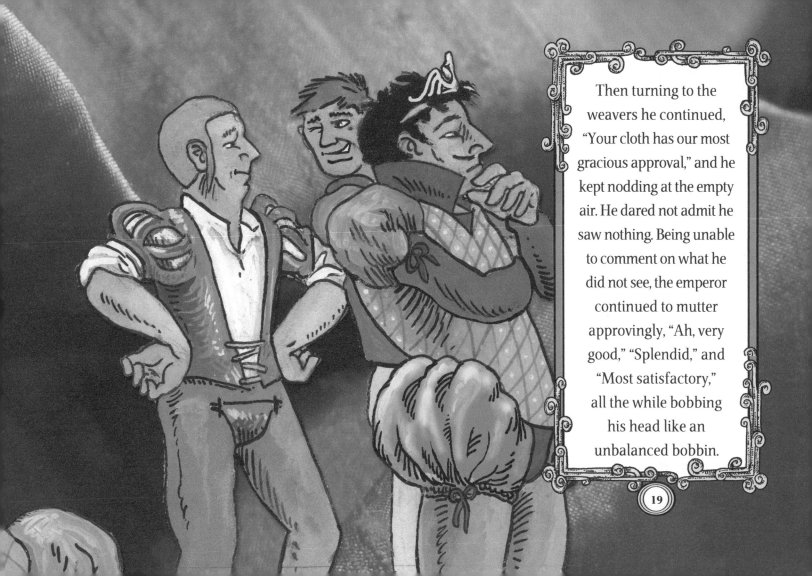

Then turning to the weavers he continued, "Your cloth has our most gracious approval," and he kept nodding at the empty air. He dared not admit he saw nothing. Being unable to comment on what he did not see, the emperor continued to mutter approvingly, "Ah, very good," "Splendid," and "Most satisfactory," all the while bobbing his head like an unbalanced bobbin.

The courtiers who had not been there before stared studiously at the spot where the cloth *should* have been, and they, too, praised the transparent textiles. "Splendid," "Beautiful," "Excellent." Everyone rejoiced, so the emperor gave the two men the title of Imperial Court Weavers right then and there.

For the rest of that day and the rest of the night the thieves continued pretending to work on the emperor's new clothes and burned more than sixteen candles.

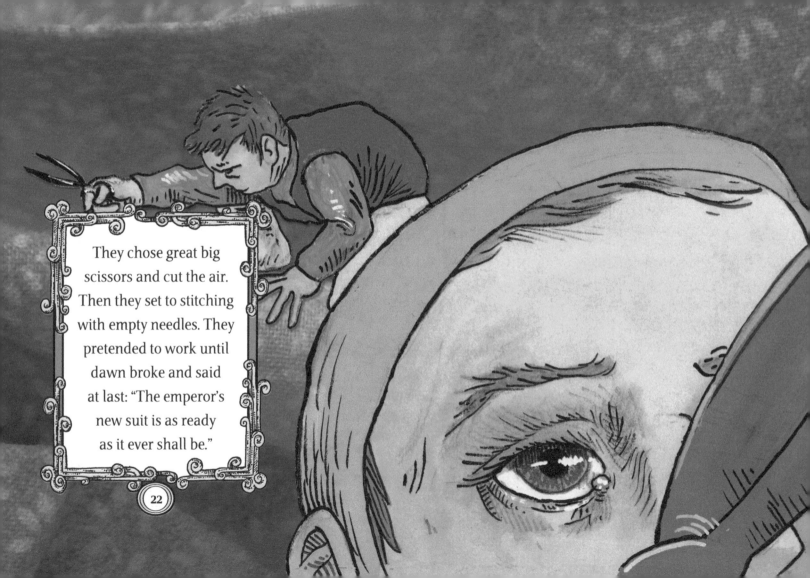

They chose great big
scissors and cut the air.
Then they set to stitching
with empty needles. They
pretended to work until
dawn broke and said
at last: "The emperor's
new suit is as ready
as it ever shall be."

The emperor and his noblemen arrived in the hall and the two deceivers lifted their arms up as if they were holding something. "See ... here are the clothes! And, Emperor, there is one more trait of this cloth we must tell you about: The beautiful clothing is as light as a cobweb. While wearing even the entire ensemble, you will feel as if you have nothing at all on your body."

"May we assist your fashionable Highness in putting on these grand new clothes?" the swindlers asked. The emperor removed his clothes, and the men helped him into his new suit. When they finally said that the dressing had finished, the emperor turned around in front of his huge mirror—pretending to admire his new clothes.

"How wonderful they look! How fine they fit!" said all the courtiers. "What a beautiful pattern! What fine colors!"
"Do these new clothes not suit me well?" the emperor asked as he turned once more in front of the mirror. "Never have I seen better looking clothes, nor worn anything that felt so light and airy."

Then the emperor said, "I am ready to show myself to the people. Let us have a parade to display my new clothes." Two servants were summoned to the hall where the emperor stood in his birthday suit. They were told to carry the long train that was supposed to be behind the emperor. They did not dare to look stupid by saying that they saw nothing to carry.

26

Then the emperor marched out, and all the people along the road started cheering: "How remarkable are the emperor's new clothes! What beautiful colors! Such a fine pattern! How it fits him!" No one dared to let on that they could not see the outfit, for that would have shown that they were not well-suited for their work—or were, in fact, very stupid.

As the emperor paraded by, one boy tugged his father's coat and shouted, "DADDY, WHY IS THE EMPEROR WEARING NO CLOTHES?"

"Did you hear what the child said?" the people whispered, and quickly the story spread.

The crowd laughed. The pretending ended. "The emperor has nothing on at all!" The emperor realized that what the people said must be true, but he thought to himself, *"I must bear up to the end."* So the emperor lifted his head higher as he marched on. And the two servants gripped tighter than ever on the cloak that never existed.

29

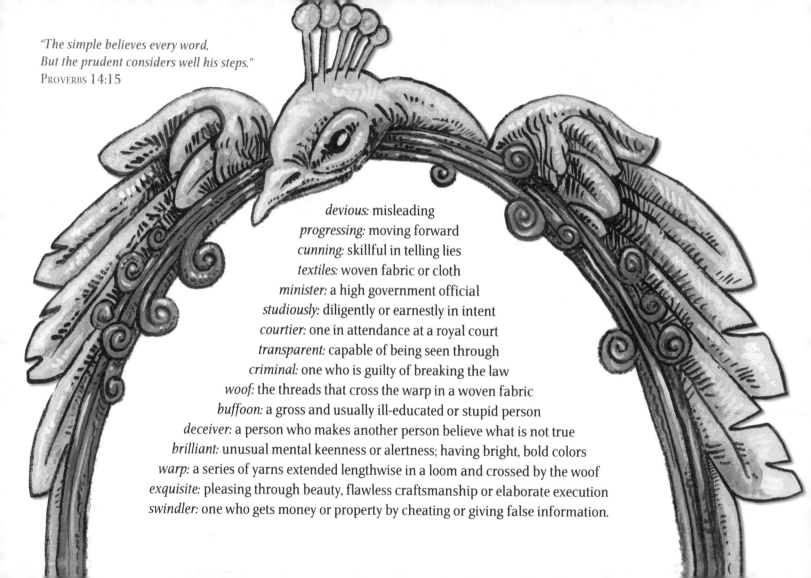

"The simple believes every word,
But the prudent considers well his steps."
PROVERBS 14:15

devious: misleading
progressing: moving forward
cunning: skillful in telling lies
textiles: woven fabric or cloth
minister: a high government official
studiously: diligently or earnestly in intent
courtier: one in attendance at a royal court
transparent: capable of being seen through
criminal: one who is guilty of breaking the law
woof: the threads that cross the warp in a woven fabric
buffoon: a gross and usually ill-educated or stupid person
deceiver: a person who makes another person believe what is not true
brilliant: unusual mental keenness or alertness; having bright, bold colors
warp: a series of yarns extended lengthwise in a loom and crossed by the woof
exquisite: pleasing through beauty, flawless craftsmanship or elaborate execution
swindler: one who gets money or property by cheating or giving false information.